PUBLISHER'S NOTE

—

It's a joy rarely experienced to discover a new classic. Here is a book that
offers just that. Created in Sweden over sixty years ago, *The Cantankerous Crow*
struck a new note in children's picture books. To this day it startles us with
its ingenuity and charms us with its warmth and humor. I discovered a
rather battered copy of the original Swedish edition, lovingly scrawled over in
pencil by the child to whom it was inscribed in 1953, in a second-hand bookshop
in Gothenburg some years ago. I realized immediately that here was something
special that cried out to be enjoyed by a whole new generation of readers.
I hope you enjoy the discovery as much as I did.

Roger Thorp

The
Cantankerous Crow

by LENNART HELLSING and POUL STRØYER

There once lived the queerest family of crows
deep in a forest as everyone knows.
There was a crow father and a crow mother,
and four crow sisters and a crow brother.

CAW-CAW

One of the sisters sang a caw-caw song,
but everyone thought that it sounded wrong.

The second one tried to write her name,
but crows' footprints was all it became.

The third made jam from good crowberries.

The fourth built a castle like a fairy's.

A farmer lived in this forest too,

with a garden in which his cherry trees grew.

Those cherries grew red and sweet all about,

and the brother Crow's mother told him to keep out.

Yet the naughty Crow sneaked in for a treat,

but the farmer caught him before he could eat.

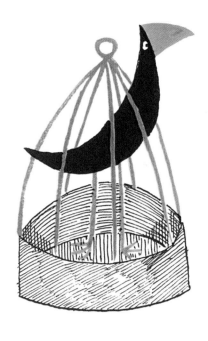

He was shut in a cage that was carefully locked

and all around him the animals flocked:

A goat and a bug and a very thin cat,

a very fat cock and a very small rat.

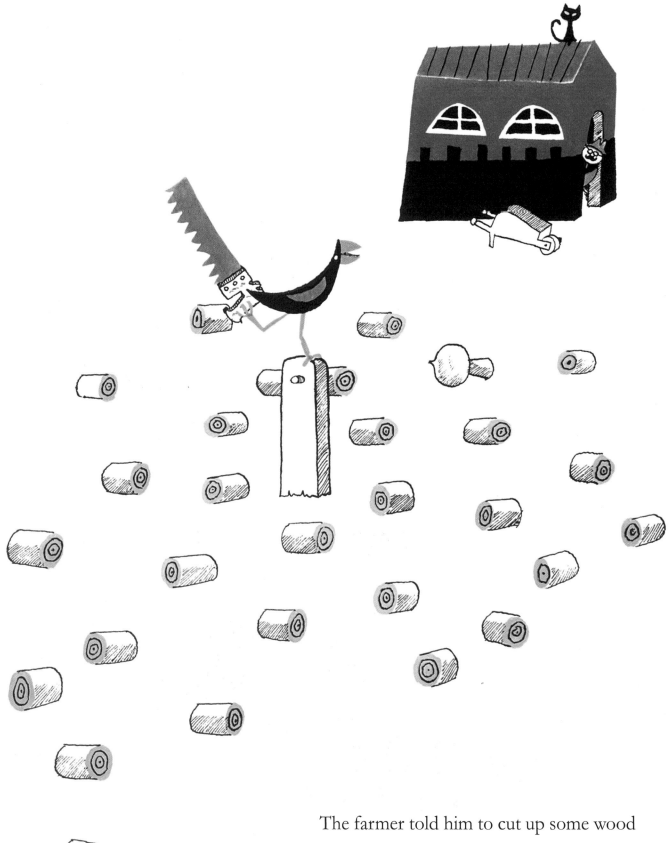

The farmer told him to cut up some wood
to earn his keep as animals should.
So he cut the flagpole down to the ground,
and chunks of firewood lay all around.

'Pump me some water,' the farmer then said.

He did it and watered the poor cat's head.

'Help sort the beans,' the farmer's wife said.

But the silly Crow fed them to the hens instead.

Then the farmer's son felt like taking a ride,

so he caught the Crow before he could hide.

He was hitched to a wagon and the boy waved his hand,

and the two of them galloped all over the land.

They rolled up and down and then all about...

...till the wagon tipped and the boy fell out.

And now the farmer was really mad,
and he said, 'This crow is very bad.
I think I'll go to the market and see
if someone will buy this bird from me.'

The farmer asked those he happened to know,

if they were thinking of buying a crow.

And everyone said: 'I might buy your honey,

but for that crow you won't get my money.'

Then the baker said, 'We might make a trade.'

And so with three cookies the farmer was paid.

The baker gave his new helper a cake,

and then he said, 'You can now help me bake.'

But soon the baker got red in the face,

for his dough was twisted all over the place.

'Stop, stop,' he cried, 'that's quite enough!

You'd better get going, you are spoiling my stuff!'

He opened the window and set the Crow free

and he flew straight home, where he wanted to be.

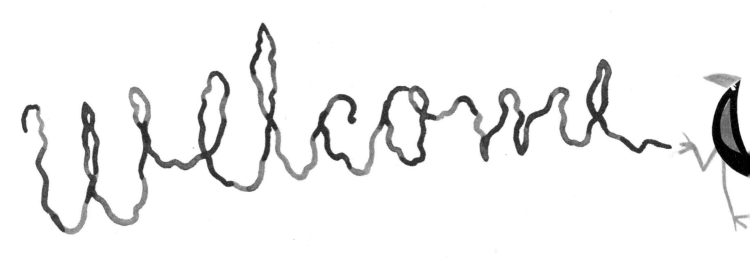

All his sisters cried, 'We've missed you so.'
And Brother Crow said, 'That's a pleasure to know.'

And the sister who always wanted to write
wrote a WELCOME sign that looked just right.

And the sister who always wanted to sing
sang him a song that was fit for a king.

And the sister who tried to cook all the time
baked him a cake that was perfectly fine.

And the sister who had a big room to rent
said, 'You can move in, it won't cost you a cent.'

Then before the Crow brother went off to bed,

he told them about the life he had led.

And the father, the mother and sisters four

lived with their brother just as before.

THE STORY BEHIND
THE CANTANKEROUS CROW

Told from memory by Lennart Hellsing (1919–2015)
to his daughter Susanna Hellsing in September 2015

After the Second World War I got to know a number of Danish authors and
visual artists who were pioneering a new artistic approach to picture books.
Among them was Poul Strøyer (1923–96), an artist living in Copenhagen.
In 1946 Strøyer moved to Stockholm where he was commissioned
to work for the *Stockholms-Tidningen*, where I was a journalist.

One day in the editor's office, I spotted a miniature no bigger than a matchstick.
It had been drawn by Strøyer. I sought out the Danish illustrator. We found that we
had a great deal in common and became firm friends. For a long time I had been
thinking to myself: "Why are there so many bad picture books in the world?
Good pictures don't cost any more than bad pictures." With this in mind we decided
to co-write a book for children. It was called *Summa Summarum [All in all]*, and was
published in 1950. It was Strøyer's debut in the field of children's books and
it was nominated as best picture book of the year.

Spurred on by this success, we created *The Cantankerous Crow* for a children's book
competition held in 1951 by *Folket i Bild*, a Swedish illustrated news magazine, where it
received a special mention. It was inspired by folktales about crows who mischievously lie in
wait for country folk. The book was subsequently published in Sweden in 1953 and the first
English-language edition was published in New York in 1959. I went on to publish over a
hundred books for children, including a further fourteen with Poul Strøyer.

In the late 1950s Strøyer became an illustrator for *Dagens Nyheter*, the biggest daily
newspaper in Sweden, where he worked until his death. He was also an accomplished painter,
and his work is represented in many museums, including the Nationalmuseum in Stockholm.

It is a particular pleasure to see this very special book that we made
together republished for a new generation of children.

First published in the United Kingdom in 2016 by
Thames & Hudson Ltd, 181A High Holborn,
London WC1V 7QX
www.thamesandhudson.com

First published in New York by McDowell / Obolensky
This edition first published in 2016 in hardcover in the
United States of America by Thames & Hudson Inc.,
500 Fifth Avenue, New York, New York 10110
thamesandhudsonusa.com

Original Swedish title DEN KRÅNGLIGA KRÅKAN
First published by Rabén & Sjögren, Sweden.
Published by agreement with Rabén & Sjögren Agency.
Text © Lennart Hellsing 1953 and 2008.
Illustrations © Poul Strøyer 1953 and 2008.
Adapted from the Swedish by Nancy and Edward Maze.
'The Story Behind *The Cantankerous Crow*' translated from
the Swedish by Rita Eustace.

British Library Cataloguing-in-Publication Data
A catalogue record for this book is available from the British Library

Library of Congress Catalog Card Number 2015959545

ISBN   978-0-500-65079-0

Printed and bound in China